Legacy of Exiled Prince: Book 1

A Progression Fantasy

contents

CHAPTER 1: AWAKENING

F ootsteps echoed in the darkness, followed by the
knock on the prison cells. A knock that stabbed into
every prisoner's heart, making them question what kind of
horror they might be facing tonight. The sound of metal
against metal reverberated through the dank corridors, ac-
companied by the soft hiss of torch flames.

Everyone huddled in their cells, many of them stum-
bling backward, pressing their backs on the moss coat-
ed prison walls in hope the warden wouldn't see them
tonight. Whimpers and prayers filled the stale air as shadows danced across the stone floor.

However, nothing escaped from the eyes of the all-see-
ing warden, Gra'pa, as he loved to call himself. His boots
clicked methodically against the flagstones, each step de-

liberate and menacing. Some said he was a monster who fed on the fear felt by the prisoners, and some said he just enjoyed the fear on their faces.

No one knew the answer.

"Who's feeling scared tonight?" His gravelly voice carried through the corridor. "Perhaps we'll have some entertainment, yes?"

In the dark dungeons under the city of Palor, no one feared the king more than they feared Gra'pa.

Stories of his cruelty had become whispered legends among the inmates, tales of midnight interrogations from which only the husk of a prisoner returned.

But there was an exception today. A young man, haggard, his skin touching his bones, sat near the edge of the cell, holding the scrappy metal bars with his scarred hands. He could smell the piss and copper of the prison cells, and taste the salty air whenever he opened his mouth. Rats scurried past his feet, their tiny claws scratching against the stone floor. It wasn't ideal, and he would prefer a morning sunlight any day, but he was living with whatever he got in the dungeon prison.

"You seem awfully brave tonight, boy," Gra'pa sneered, pausing before his cell. "Or perhaps you're simply too far gone to care anymore? Your death is only ten days away, my beloved Prince."

Aston Wrenfield hadn't felt alive in the last three months like he felt today, but it wasn't the real Aston Wrenfield, but someone who had transmigrated from the Earth into this body of a prince. His fingers tightened around the bars as he met the warden's gaze, surprising himself with his own defiance.

Though much of the original Aston's past remained a fog, one fact stood crystal clear: in ten days, he would face the executioner. The execution order had been signed and sealed, its weight hanging over him like a shadow. Yet somehow, that knowledge gave him a strange sort of freedom. After all, what more could they take from a dead man walking?

A headache threatened to take over him as he tried to access the clouded memories of the original prince. So he just stopped accessing them.

"Your silence won't save you, princeling," Gra'pa chuckled, tapping his metal rod against the bars. "Ten days is a long time to suffer. Shall I tell you a secret?" Gra'pa pushed his nose through the metal bars, the stench of his breath assaulted Aston.

Aston chuckled, a voice full of menace. "You can't rape me, Gra'pa. I'm a prince. Albeit locked inside the dungeon, I'm still a prince."

"Nine days, and the sweet ass of yours will be mine." Gra'pa licked the bars with his tongue. "Before they kill you, no one will care if you are ass-virgin or not. They will watch you die with horror on your face, but no one will notice the reason behind that horror."

Aston's fingers tightened on the bars, Earth-born instincts warring with this body's ingrained fears. He'd faced death before, in another life, but never quite like this.

Aston stared into Gra'pa's eyes, his gaze unflinching against the predatory gleam. The dank air of the dungeon carried whispers of this man's reputation - this ass-loving motherfucker had violated everyone trapped here. From the way the guards averted their eyes and even the prison dogs cowered, Aston bet none had escaped his perverted obsession.

However, he couldn't touch Aston nor Aston could do anything to him, and Aston used this false sense of security to draw him closer to the cell, watching as Gra'pa's rancid breath fogged the metal bars.

With lightning speed, Aston thrust his arms through the gaps and seized Gra'pa's thick neck, fingers locking into a vice-like grip. The rough stubble scratched against his palms as he squeezed.

Gra'pa's eyes flickered with a cascade of emotions - surprise, shock, and finally raw horror as Aston's long nails dug deep into his flesh, piercing through skin and severing delicate nerves. Warm blood trickled down Aston's fingers.

"How dare you!" Gra'pa shouted, his voice echoing off the stone walls. The outrage in his tone stemmed not from pain, but from the sheer audacity of his prisoner's defiance. Until now, his mere presence had commanded terror - Aston had witnessed hardened criminals piss in their pants under Gra'pa's gaze. But Aston wasn't like them. He'd seen worse on Earth, and Gra'pa deserved every bit of pain. If only Aston hadn't been weakened by days of imprisonment, he could have employed the lethal neck hold he'd learned in his previous life.

"Not so tough now, are you?" Aston sneered, twisting his nails deeper into the tender flesh. His weak hands cried in pain from days of disuse, muscles trembling with the strain, but the years of his practice sessions memory kicked in like muscle memory from another life. He held Gra'pa with the least power he needed, applying just enough pressure to maintain control - a technique he'd perfected during countless assignments. Even in his weakened state, some skills never truly faded.

"Motherfucker. I'll kill you!" Gra'pa's initial shock transformed into murderous rage. He wrenched himself free and thrust his metal rod through the bars with deadly intent. Aston's muscles screamed as he twisted away like a shadow, the rod whooshing past his ear with a sharp whistle. The close call sent his heart racing - one hit from that weapon would have ended him right there.

"You missed," Aston taunted, tasting copper in his mouth as he smiled.

"I'm going to rape you tonight, motherfucker. I'll shred your skin and make a ring of your bones around my neck." Gra'pa licked his lips as he searched for the keys.

"Are you searching for these?" Aston jangled the bunch of keys he had managed to steal from Gra'pa's waist during the shocking attack. His fingers trembled slightly around the cold metal, but he kept his voice steady. It had been a fortunate grab, pure chance really, and Aston wasn't foolish enough to count on such fortune again. Still, these keys were now his bargaining chip - perhaps the only thing standing between him and a brutal death in this cesspit.

"Give them to me, Aston. Else I will break the lock and kill you tonight. Don't you test my patience, ant."

"And join me in hell a few days later? What do you think my father will do when he learns his son, a prince, died in the prison?" Aston's voice carried just the right amount of aristocratic disdain.

"I'll make it look like an accident." Gra'pa's scarred face twisted into a sneer. "I've killed many. Even a noble son, and no one cared." He wiped the blood from his neck, but he didn't notice what Aston had mixed into his blood with his fingers.

"Because he wasn't a prince." Aston snapped back. "My father has to answer to the church, people and to keep his respect among his subjects, he will burn down the entire prison. If you don't believe this, then ask your master, Bathos." Aston chuckled, though his insides churned with anxiety and pain. It had been two days since he ate anything, but that wouldn't stop him today. He had rehearsed this conversation countless times in his head, mapping out each possible response. So far, the pieces were falling exactly where he needed them.

"And you fucking need the keys because my brothers and sisters will visit me to fool the common people about how much they love me despite my crimes." Aston added to his threat. One of those fuckers had trapped the original Aston, but he didn't know who among them.

"Give me the keys, and I promise I will spare your ass." Gra'pa gripped the metal bars, pushing his face through them, his eyes trying to burn Aston alive.

Only if eyes could kill.

"Bring Sir Rodric to visit me, and I'll pass on the keys to you." Aston kept his voice level, though speaking the name made his mouth go dry. Everything hinged on this request.

Sir Rodric was the only man who could get him out of this mess, and help him meet his own father, the king.

Gra'pa chuckled. "Are you nuts, Aston? Why would sir Rodric will visit you? He is the main guard of the king's security, and he has better things to do than to visit a fallen prince. And I can't even reach him."

"Just tell him that I've the Calling of the Ancient, and a sheer amount of gold hidden somewhere only I know."

Gra'pa's eyes flickered with greed. Even in the dim light of the cell, Aston saw it. Despite having five blank magic portals, he could still see through the darkness. It was a basic ability, and he had mastered it even before his awakening.

"Gra'pa. This is beyond your paygrade. But if you help Sir Rodric gain a large amount of gold, he might spare a coin or two at you. Don't even think of getting the information from me. Do you understand, motherfucker?" Aston whispered, barely audible to anyone but him and Gra'pa.

Gra'pa froze. For his betterment, he knew he couldn't get the information out of Aston and use it to collect all the gold if it was there.

"I'll see what I can do." Gra'pa turned back. "But if you don't hand over the keys by tomorrow, I'll break the cell and let the hungry dogs fuck you."

"Put some Healing Powder on your neck else the poison will burn through your skin tonight. If you get Sir Rodric here by tomorrow, I'll give you the antidote name."

"A poison?"

Aston chuckled, letting the fear settle in Gra'pa's eyes. No way he would tell what poison he used to injure Gra'pa. Not even if he had to die for it.

CHAPTER 2: BISHOP'S STAND

R odric

"Gra'pa is dead. He was poisoned with mana-poison," Sir Rodric said, rising up from his ceremonial bow before Bishop Aganstha.

With a respectful nod, he stepped back and stood next to a stone pillar, his rightful place, as per Bishop. From here her devotees could gaze on the arms of the Bishop sitting on the high chair of the church hall. But given Rodric's height, he could even gaze beyond her and look at the stars shining from the window behind her.

"A mana-poison?" Bishop Aganstha's brows arched up in a furrow. Her fingers tightened around her ceremonial staff. "Where did he get one? Such potions are strictly regulated by the church."

"I don't know. I'm not sure." Rodric stroked his long beard. "Gra'pa died before I could talk with him, and his healer mentioned he kept saying prince Aston wanted to meet me."

Bishop Aganstha rose and walked to the side table where the servants kept her teapot filled. Her silk robes whispered against the stone floor, the sound echoing in the vast hall.

Rodric watched her robed figure pour herself a cup of tea, which smelled of jasmine, while forcing a smile on his face. He had been to this place for the countless times, but the woman had never asked him for a cup of tea despite being an equally strong magician like her. Was it her age, or the church's authority that infused arrogance in her old bones?

"What are you planning to do as your prisons are corrupted by the Dark Order frantic? If they can get poison inside the prison, I bet they can get the prince out as well," she said in a plain tone, but every word stung like poison. Her wrinkled fingers traced the rim of her teacup, the gentle scraping sound adding weight to her words.

"Gra'pa was my man, and he made sure nothing could get through the door of the dungeon." Rodric's deep voice resonated against the stone walls. "I'll wipe the guards and install new ones, so no mishap like this will happen. I'll make sure to punish Prince and make it as an example for others." His eyes narrowed as he spoke, his long beard quivering with each word.

"Prince is a small pawn. Don't punish him. In fact, meet him." Bishop Aganstha sat back in her chair and sipped her tea, the jasmine aroma wafting between them like an invisible curtain.

"Meet the prince?" Rodric ran a hand over his bald head, his muscular frame tensing. "It's not appropriate, Bishop. King would execute me for meeting his treacherous son."

"Play it smart, Rodric." She set down her cup with a soft clink. "Put it through the king's mouth. Tell him Dark Order will try to free him once he is out of the dungeon, and it is our chance to catch them"

Rodric licked his lips, tasting the bitter tang of uncertainty. This was a good plan, but there was a flaw. The prince. Bishop Aganstha, the emissary of the church, had been fooled many times by a mere prince, and he might be up to something once more. She seemed to be sent here to catch the criminals, but he suspected she had some other motives.

"Prince is not a fool." Rodric's fingers drummed against his thigh. "He had prepared enough evidence to put me behind bars. Don't underestimate him, Bishop. He would know we will keep a trail on him, and grab the Dark Order bastards if they try to free him," he said, his century of experience weighing heavily in his voice. That bastard prince grew up in front of his eyes, and what he lacked in magic, he made it up with his immense knowledge and wits.

"That you will check." Bishop Aganstha's lips curved into a knowing smile. "If he has something to trade, you might find his offer attractive." The steam from her tea curled upward like serpents in the cold air.

"No way." Rodric chuckled, the sound hollow against the stone walls. "I like money, but I like my life more. There is nothing Prince Aston can trade for his life. The king will not allow it." He stood up, his shadow stretching across the floor like a giant's. It was an impossible thing, and if Prince Aston had a foolish hope of trading something, then he would only get disappointed.

The bishop's silence spoke volumes as she watched him over the rim of her teacup, her eyes glinting with secrets yet untold.

CHAPTER 3: MEETING

Two days had passed since Aston sent a desperate message through Gra'pa, but the warden hadn't come back, nor had the meager scraps they sent as a meal made their way to the prison cells. The stench of piss and human waste had grown unbearable in the humid air, intensified by the complete lack of ventilation, making each breath a struggle against nausea. The stone walls seemed to sweat, adding to the oppressive atmosphere.

Aston was waiting, his nerves fraying with each passing hour, but no one came to ask him anything - not the guards, not the interrogators, not even the usual prison staff. The wheezing in his lungs had grown worse, the damp conditions exacerbating Aston's condition until each breath rattled painfully in his chest. Dark spots danced at the edges of his vision whenever he moved too quickly. At this rate, he might not survive the seven days until his scheduled execution, his body giving out before the executioner could finish the job.

Prisoners were wailing for food, some even pushing their asses out through the rusty bars in the hope Gra'pa would come and give them food. The desperation in their voices echoed off the stone walls, creating a haunting chorus of human misery.

"Please, just a crust of bread!" one prisoner sobbed, his skeletal hands reaching through the bars. "I will do anything."

"Shut your trap!" another prisoner growled, followed by the sound of scuffling in the darkness.

Aston never thought a single meal could bring the whore out of these prisoners. But then again, he hadn't been in a prison back on Earth. A couple of encounters with the cops in his youth - mostly street fights and petty theft - had straightened him out. Later, he'd joined a security force company and became a consultant himself, teaching others how to prevent the very things he once did.

Footsteps echoed in the darkness, the steady tap-tap-tap growing louder. For the first time since he woke up in the dead body of Aston Wrenfield, he saw the prisoners not wailing in fear. Instead, they pressed against their cell doors, eyes gleaming with desperate hunger. They were waiting for the food they thought they deserved.

"Get ready, boys!" someone called out. "Gra'pa's coming with our feast!"

Aston thought otherwise, his security training kicking in as he assessed their situation. It was better to die than getting raped in these piss-filled cells, or succumb to the moss-coated walls which harbored god knows what kind of diseases. The green-black growth pulsed faintly in the dim light, almost seeming alive.

However, the rats were more deadly. Poisonous. Their red eyes glowed in the darkness as they scurried past, and one of them had magic - the same creature whose venom had killed the original Aston Wrenfield and allowed the Aston from Earth to transmigrate into this body.

"The rats," he whispered to himself, watching one scurry past his cell. "They're not normal."

How that happened, Aston had no idea. The last time he recalled, he was sleeping next to his girlfriend in their apartment in Chicago, and then he woke up in this half-dead body, infested with poison. The poison had mysteriously cured itself once he woke up - another unexplained phenomenon in this strange world.

Was he summoned by gods, a magician, or a priest? No one knew. But one thing he knew was that this world had magic, and people had magic portals inside their bodies from which they harness the power - mana. He could feel it now, a warm pulse in his chest, like a second heartbeat waiting to be understood.

However, Aston's magical potential remained frustratingly out of reach. He lacked the fundamental knowledge to transform his five blank portals into a functional spell circle. As a commoner, this deficiency would be a setback; as a prince, it was catastrophic.

Two guards stopped outside of his cells, their metal rods tapping rhythmically on the stone ground until everyone in the dungeon corridor turned silent. The old man in the opposite cell hid back into the dark shadows to hide from the guards. The dim torchlight cast long shadows through the iron bars, making their armored silhouettes seem more imposing than they were.

"Prince Aston, we are taking you out. Stay in the corner. If you raise your hand we will be forced to tie you with rope and drag you with us." One of the guards with a scurry face said in a polite tone, his words formal but dripping with barely concealed contempt. Despite addressing royalty, he lacked any semblance of decency toward the fallen prince, treating him like common filth.

Well, Aston wasn't a prince anymore. He was labeled as a rapist, wife-stealer and a stain on humanity. How quickly they'd turned on him, forgetting his status and breeding like it had never existed. The accusations felt like physical weights pressing down on his shoulders.

He cared for nothing. He wasn't the original Aston, nor he cared for such accusations.

Aston got up, his wobbly legs barely managing to hold his own weight. After sitting cross-legged in this position for more than a few hours on the cold stone floor, he had lost all feeling in his legs, and with his weakened, malnourished body it would take at least a minute for circulation to return. His muscles screamed in protest as pins and needles shot through his limbs.

The second guard opened the door with a master key and grabbed Aston, guiding him outside of the dungeon. The first sun-ray after days of darkness felt like an angel's blessing. His skin tingled with the warmth, reminding him how much he'd missed this simple pleasure. Vitamin D3 might be overrated on Earth, but here, the sunlight was precious currency.

It was a blessing. More than a blessing - it was life itself.

His eyes watered as he squinted against the harsh light, raising a shackled hand to shield his face. The long dusty road swam in his vision, a blur of browns and greens. If he could get a cup of cappuccino, he would be set for the day. But such earthly comforts were beyond his reach now.

"Is Gra'pa dead already?" Aston asked, his voice raspy from disuse. He couldn't keep his eyes open for long, so he just closed them and let the guards take him wherever they wanted him to go.

The guard with the scarred face shifted uncomfortably. "He barely survived. Someone poked him with a magic-poison, and the priest is treating him. Touch and go, they say."

"Where are you taking me, boys?" Aston's legs trembled beneath him as they walked. Surprisingly, the road had very less gravel and when he opened his eyes, he saw they had walked away from the road to dungeon and moving over a paved road.

"Sir Rodric is expecting you," the main guard whispered, nervously glancing over his shoulder. "So you better wash yourself from the filth and meet him with a presence of mind." His grip tightened on Aston's arm as he steered him away from the main route, weaving through narrow alleys and shadowed corners until they reached the rear entrance of a tavern.

A prisoner, marked for execution, entering a tavern through the back doors - the irony wasn't lost on him.

Aston sneered at the atrocity. He expected this from the original Aston's memories. Everyone here was corrupted, and Sir Rodric was the capital's crown prince of corruption. The original Aston had wanted to bring him down along with the other pests eating away at the city, but he'd fallen for a honey trap instead.

Poor fellow. The original Aston would probably cough up blood if he knew his replacement was seeking help from the very man he'd sworn to destroy.

"Get into the bath, and wear the plain clothes left next to the tub." The scarred guard shoved him into a spacious room dominated by an oversized empty bathtub. Warm water flowed from an ornate carving in the corner, steam rising in lazy spirals as it filled the tub.

"Don't try anything stupid," the second guard warned, hand on his sword hilt. "We'll be right outside."

Aston managed a weak smile. "Wouldn't dream of it."

With trembling fingers, he tore away his tattered clothes, the fabric sticky with grime and sweat. He eased himself into the tub slowly, his body too weak for any sudden movements. The warm water embraced his naked form, and he had to bite back a moan of relief as it soothed his battered muscles. Each ripple felt like a healer's touch, washing away days of accumulated filth and pain.

"Heaven," he whispered, closing his eyes. "Just five more minutes of this, and I might actually feel human again." Aston closed his eyes, feeling the mana in the surrounding entering him through the pores. It wasn't evident in prison, but he could sense it the moment he stepped out of the dungeon.

"Enjoying your bath, prince?" A deep groovy voice jolted Aston from his peaceful reverie. His eyes snapped open to find a bald and naked Sir Rodric had somehow silently entered the tub, his evaluating gaze traveling over Aston's form with unsettling intensity.

"Sir Rodric, I never thought you would possess the same motivation as that pest, Gra'pa." Aston kept his voice steady despite his racing heart, refusing to show weakness.

Sir Rodric chuckled, the sound echoing off the stone walls as he lowered his feet into the tub with deliberate slowness. His long beard floated on the water's surface like seaweed. Despite his youthful appearance and impressively muscled physique, Aston knew the truth - the man before him had lived for over a century, preserved by the magic that flowed through this world like blood through veins.

"Prince, you are overestimating my courage." Sir Rodric's lips curved into what might have been a smile.

"Then why meet me in this tub? Aren't you afraid of soiling your precious skin?" Aston met the man's dark brown eyes unflinchingly. Though Sir Rodric was corrupt to his core, Aston felt no fear. The political calculations were clear - if Aston died before his scheduled execution,

Sir Rodric would face severe consequences. The man was too cunning to risk such a move. If he wanted to kill Aston, his best bet would have been Gra'pa - a disposable pawn.

Aston splashed his face with clean water, marveling inwardly at his own political knowledge. These weren't his original thoughts or memories, yet since his arrival in this world, his mind had sharpened, gaining an edge of subtle sophistication he'd never possessed before.

"I'm afraid of many things, Prince." Sir Rodric's voice dropped lower, more intimate. "But I'm not afraid of meeting a man in the most intimate settings. I think it brings out the rare honesty among men. Don't you think so, Prince Aston?" He arched his brows meaningfully, then tapped the water's surface. A pulse of magic rippled outward from his torso, pushing the dirty water away from his skin in a perfect circle.

"And I thought you liked to get your hands dirty, Sir Rodric." Aston's chuckle held no humor. "Let's cut through the pretense. I'll give you fifty thousand gold coins for reliable information about Lady Evelin and a meeting with the king."

Sir Rodric's expression darkened as he rose from the water, muscles coiling like a predator preparing to strike. The tip of his extended finger began to glow an ominous red, pulsing with the fire magic he was infamous for. Water dripped from his form as magical heat began to distort the air around them.

"Do you treat me as a fool, Prince Aston?" The words came out as a dangerous whisper, steam rising from where the droplets fell from his finger.

Was he going to use his magic on Aston?

CHAPTER 4:
DISAPPOINTMENT

Magic was fundamental to this world, woven into its very fabric like threads in a cloth. People were generally born with mana in their bodies, flowing through their bodies, infusing them with vitality and power. The first awakening process allowed them to open mana portals, shimmering doorways of pure energy that would transform into intricate spell circles through the second awakening. Those blessed with a mana portal were known as seedlings, carrying the potential for greater power, while those who successfully formed spell circles earned the respected title of awakened.

Aston Wrenfield's awakening ceremony had been a spectacle of initial promise and subsequent devastation.

Five mana portals had burst forth from his body, their potential sending the entire kingdom in a tremor and celebration.

However, the palace of glass crumbled in the second awakening done a few hours after where none of the mana portal transformed into a spell circle.

The mighty, all-loved prince turned into a trash. The whispers began, then the looks of pity, and finally the barely concealed contempt. In the span of a few hours, he had gone from being the pride of Valtoria to its greatest disappointment.

Aston from Earth possessed all the theoretical knowledge inherited from the original prince, every detail crystal clear in his mind. But the theory felt hollow now as he stood before Sir Rodric, watching the old knight's fingers trace patterns in the air that sparked with dangerous energy.

"Sir Rodric, are you showing me your flashy spell?" Aston asked, continuing to scrub behind his ears where stubborn dirt clung like a reminder of his time in the prison. The warm water cascading over him had managed to wash away most of the dust and moss, but without proper soap, he felt far from clean.

Sir Rodric's eyes crinkled with amusement beneath his thick brows. "Prince Aston, I never thought you would have grown balls to stand in front of a magician."

"I've grown many more things, Sir Rodric. Sanity, maturity and knowledge." Aston rubbed the dirt away from his navel.

"Isn't it far too late? You could have been enjoying inside your own bedchamber right now rather than standing filthy in front of me. Begging for your life." Sir Rodric's finger glowed brighter and brighter, like a molten rock about to burst with fire.

Aston sighed, his mind wandering to his luxurious bathroom back on Earth, with its gleaming fixtures and modern conveniences. He could almost feel the smooth porcelain of his oversized tub, smell the expensive bath oils, and see Jessica lounging in the bubbles, her playful smile inviting him in. The memory stung worse than any spell could.

"Fuck it, Sir Rodric. Why don't you just kill me?" Aston got up and walked toward Sir Rodric with a crazy thought, water dripping from his body into the dirty tub. This might be just a dream, and if he died, then he would be back next to his girlfriend. He could pull her warm arm over his cold body, and they could make love. Maybe it was time to settle down. A few days in the dream prison had straightened him up.

Sir Rodric's brows arched upward, his index finger turning hotter and hotter, the air around it shimmering like a heat mirage.

His eyes were sending a warning to Aston, but he didn't care about it anymore.

As Aston stepped closer, he could smell the vapors wafting from the hot finger, reminiscent of a blacksmith's forge.

Without hesitation, Aston pressed his forehead on the red finger and a sizzling sensation spread through his skin, a smell of burning skin and flesh wafted around, and a deep pain throbbed through his face. The agony was unlike anything he'd experienced in his stint on earth during security assignments, even during the worst confrontations.

"Fuck, you are crazy." Sir Rodric dropped his finger and leaped out of the bathtub in a rush, water splashing everywhere. He quickly donned a robe placed at the edge, his movements sharp with concern. "You are crazier than they whisper about you." He walked out, his wet footprints marking his path. "Come out after scrubbing yourself. We will talk."

Aston stood there, fear surging through his mind, his reflection in the rippling water showing an angry red mark between his eyes. Did he just think this was all a dream, and put his head on the gun's point? His security training screamed at his recklessness.

Fuck! This wasn't a dream, and a burned patch of skin between his eyes told him the truth. The throbbing pain pulsed with each heartbeat, a constant reminder of his newfound reality.

Then he saw blue and purple everywhere. It was mana. He had heard about it, and he could see it once more. But it was useless for him.

Ten minutes and an intense scrub later, Aston sat across Sir Rodric on a plush fabric chair, his skin still pink from the vigorous cleaning. In front of him lay a table full of delicacies: succulent cuts of meat, roasted pork dripping with savory juices, steaming white rice, and earthen jars filled with fantastic smelling ale that made his mouth water despite his reservations.

However, Aston touched nothing on the table, especially not the wine, his security training screaming caution at every turn. The original prince didn't have a good capacity for alcohol, and even though Aston had earned his reputation as a tank when it came to drinking back on Earth, he wasn't sure how this body would handle its liquor. The last thing he needed was to lose his edge in this precarious situation.

He wasn't ready to take any chance.

"Eat away, prince." Sir Rodric pointed at the plates. "It's much better than the shit you are eating inside the prison. Although it can't match the taste of food cooked in the royal chambers, I can at least offer you some solace and change of taste." He picked up a piece of juicy meat with a metal fork and placed it inside his mouth, his long tongue wrapping around the brown meat in an almost serpentine fashion.

"Sir Rodric, I came bearing gifts, but it looks like you don't intend to accept those." Aston placed his elbows on the table, leaning a little forward. The red dot on his forehead was screaming in pain, throbbing with each heartbeat, but this was more important than any other injury he'd sustained.

Sir Rodric chewed on the piece of meat more than an average human would, his jaw working methodically as his dark brown eyes studied Aston with careful consideration.

"Prince Aston, let me get straight to the point." He swallowed deliberately before continuing. "You crusaded against the corrupt officials of the city when you couldn't get your magic working."

Aston nodded, maintaining eye contact. There was no point in hiding what the original prince wanted to do. In this situation, he had nothing to hide.

"I know for sure one of the names in those documents belonged to me." Sir Rodric drank from a glass filled with red ale.

"I just need the information on lady Evelina and a meeting with the king, my father."

"Which you can ask yourself when you meet the majesty before your execution." Sir Rodric put the glass back on the table.

"Sir Rodric, we don't need a political advisor to tell us it won't happen if I ask nicely. As a head of the king's security, you can get me in and get me out, and given my position, I doubt my father will blame you for anything." Aston's voice carried the practiced confidence of someone used to negotiating difficult situations.

"He won't blame me, but execute me the next moment. I can't do it." Sir Rodric shook his head, his long beard swaying with the motion. His calloused fingers drummed against his glass. "You are asking too much for a mere fifty thousand gold, Prince."

"You can plead my case to him, and I'm sure you have your ways to get him to agree to meet him. I'm his legitimate son, after all, and not a bastard from a whore he visits every other day." The words came out sharp and deliberate, each one chosen to provoke a reaction.

Sir Rodric tapped on the table with his thick fingers, creating a tense atmosphere. The sound echoed through the room like a countdown, and the air grew heavy with unspoken threats.

"Prince, I can arrest you for treason. The words you spoke are treachery, and against the king." His dark brown eyes narrowed dangerously.

"And I'm already seven days away from my execution. You can't take away something from a man which he doesn't have, Sir Rodric," Aston replied, leaning back on the comfy chair, letting his muscles relax against the plush fabric. It had been days since his back rested peacefully on something like this, and he savored the small comfort even in this precarious moment.

"You are right. I can't take life away from you." Sir Rodric wiped his hands on a pristine white cloth before getting up. "And I prefer you die in seven days. Fifty thousand gold can buy a life, but not of a prince's life. Even if I could, I would never work with you." Sir Rodric sipped from his glass one last time. "It was nice talking with you, prince. Eat to your fill as you won't be getting anything for the next seven days. Gra'pa is almost dead, and it will only bring more trouble to your plate than any food." He walked away from the table, his face firm as stone.

There goes the only chance Aston had for survival.

CHAPTER 5: A WISE OLD MAN

Aston poked at the unidentifiable chunks of scrap food, his disgust growing with each prod. Whenever he looked at what seemed like a piece of meat, he recalled the juicy pork leg on the table of Sir Rodric - the way it had glistened in the firelight, dripping with savory juices and fragrant herbs. Compared to that piece of meat, the one he had in the dented plate looked like scraped from a dead dog's bones. It even smelled of rot and insult, the putrid aroma making his stomach churn.

Two days. Only two days remained for his execution, and yet they gave him food that even a dead corpse would refuse.

"Fucking bastards." Lifting the piece of bone, he tossed it out, and it flew through the metal bars and ended up in the opposite cell, hitting the old man sitting in the corner, eating through his own plate. The bone clattered against the stone floor, echoing in the dank corridor.

The old man with a long scrap beard glared at Aston for a moment, his button eyes narrowing in the dim light before finding out it was a piece of meat. His dusty, wrinkled face breaking into a toothless grin, and then he thanked Aston before eagerly snatching it up.

"Young man, you ought to eat if you want to live." The old man chuckled while sucking on the bone Aston had thrown at him, the wet sounds of his desperate feeding filling the space between them. "They don't feed us regular here, and when they do..." He paused to wipe his mouth with a grimy sleeve. "Well, let's just say you'll learn to appreciate even these scraps and harness mana out of it."

Aston watched as the old man devoured every last morsel, gnawing desperately at the bone until even the marrow was gone, his own stomach growling in bitter protest. He had been here almost for ten days now, and the original prince for a hundred odd days, and he hadn't seen much of this old man in the crowded dungeons. The torch light outside their cells flickered erratically, casting dancing shadows across the grimy, moisture-streaked walls which exaggerated the old man's hunched over posture into something monstrous and unsightly.

"How long have you been here?" Aston asked, pushing his plate away with a metallic scrape.

The old man's eyes grew distant, clouded with memories. "Long enough to see ten winters through that window crack," he muttered, pointing to a thin sliver in the stone wall above. Frost-laden winds whistled through the narrow opening, carrying with them the faintest shimmer of silver light. "You don't need to eat as long as you can collect the silver of mana coming out of that crack, and your position is the best to gather it." His voice turned solemn, as if a great teacher spilling the beans of wisdom.

A rat scurried across the floor between them, its tiny claws clicking against the stone.

"You mean there's enough mana here to sustain life?" Aston asked, leaning forward. Mana was life, and as long as one could absorb it, they could live a peaceful life. The people in this world lived at least hundred and fifty years by passive mana absorption.

"More than enough, if you know how to harness it," the old man replied, running his fingers through his matted beard. "But few discover this secret before starvation takes them."

Aston frowned, staring deep into the old man's eyes. Normally he wouldn't be able to see in the dark, but after the trip outside of the dungeon he had gained enhanced senses, and he could feel the traces of mana moving through the prison cells. It happened after he foolishly put his forehead against Sir Rodric's fire-finger.

The ethereal streams danced like energy threads in his vision, pale and delicate compared to the robust rivers he'd witnessed outside. Compared to the outside, they were very scarce, but he could still feel them.

A single thread of blue and purple mana entered through the crack and headed toward his cell. It was like someone had opened his eyes for the mana and he could see it everywhere.

Especially inside himself.

Aston stared inside himself, his breathing slowing as he focused inward. It was like an inner vision yogis from Earth preached about. With a thought, he could see the energy network inside his body. It moved through the entire flesh, pulsing with each heartbeat, and five places were super glowing. Two of his palms radiated like miniature suns, matched by the brilliant cores in his heart, stomach, and brain. If he wasn't wrong, those were his mana portals.

Every person was born with mana running through their energy network, and when they went through first awakening, they would open up one to three mana portals. Those were the gateways to harness the energy and cast spells. The same person would undergo second awakening a few hours later and their mana portals would give birth to spell circles, intricate patterns of power that focused and shaped the raw energy.

Unfortunately, he hadn't seen a spell circle, but he had read about them and studied them. Of course, not him, but the original prince. The knowledge sat in his mind like borrowed clothing, familiar yet not quite his own.

"You see them now, don't you?" the old man whispered, his eyes glinting in the darkness. "The portals inside you are helping you, child. Harness them and live on."

"Who are you?" Aston asked, bewildered. His fingers twitched nervously at his sides as he studied the mysterious figure. He had read the stories about the old grandpa posing as a beggar to give the protagonist a cheat skill, but he wasn't a protagonist, and the old man didn't look like a beggar.

And this wasn't a story world. This was a bloody reality, and he carried a red dot between his eyebrows to tell the tales of the reality. The mark throbbed, a constant reminder of his predicament.

"No one. I seek salvation from this prison, and I ask you to give me if you ever get out of this," the old man whispered, his weathered hands trembling as he reached toward Aston. "If you look into your portals they will take you away. Into the new world."

"How can I trust you?" Aston's voice cracked. "For all I know, you could be another illusion."

The old man's laugh was dry and brittle. "Trust your instincts, boy. Look within." the old man chuckled and began breaking the bone in between his teeth. "In bones you find juice." He chuckled like a mad-man, and Aston realized he was one.

Aston hesitated, then looked inside, deeper into the mana portal that lay in his right hand. It was a shimmering blob of mana, an outlet to the mana flowing through his body. However, he couldn't channel it anywhere. The mana bubbled on the surface of his mana portal and then settled back in, creating ripples of invisible light that only he could see. Looking at it reminded him of a documentary where he had watched the bubbling lava of a volcano, mesmerizing in its dangerous beauty.

"I can feel it," he murmured, watching the energy pulse beneath his skin like luminescent veins threading through his flesh. It was mesmerizing at the least. "But I don't know what to do with it. It's like trying to catch smoke with bare hands."

A thread of mana moved around him like a cat jumping around his owner, its ethereal form casting faint, shimmering reflections on the walls. The sight made his breath catch in his throat.

Could he control the flow of mana? The question burned in his mind.

Aston focused, his forehead creasing with concentration, and the mana flowing through his energy network reacted to his call. Though he couldn't move it in other directions, he discovered he could pause it, make it faster and push it forward, like adjusting the flow of water through a pipe. The sensation tingled through his entire body, making the hair on his arms stand on end.

"Come on," he whispered to himself. "Let's see what you can really do."

Could he control the mana outside of his body?

With trembling fingers, Aston reached out and attempted to guide a mana thread moving around him. The energy responded to his touch, bending like a ribbon in the wind.

"Fuck!" He pushed his fingers through his rough hair with his free hand.

The mana thread danced along with his fingers' movements, twisting and curling at his command. When he absorbed it into his palm, it flowed along the energy network like water finding its path downhill, eventually disappearing into the mana portal. Once it entered the portal and became his mana, it vanished from his sight, leaving only a warm, tingling sensation where it had been. The success made his heart race with possibilities.

Out of curiosity, Aston controlled another mana thread present in the air and moved it around himself, testing if it had any impact on his body, wounds, clothes and anything else. Only when it touched the poison rat, his only friend in the cell, it had a change and it entered the rat and vanished, turning into the green miasma which he had used to poison Gra'pa before.

So the rat could absorb it as well.

Aston picked another thread and moved it around his mana portal, and when it touched his mana portal, it itched into the portal like a needle making a mark on semi-liquid wax.

"Who are you? And how can you control the mana threads in the air?" The old man suddenly shouted, his body shuddering visibly.

Aston frowned. Could the old man really see him controlling the mana threads? That should be impossible, right?

"Old fool, stop shouting." A guard stepped in and poked the old man with his metal rod.

"Ignore him. He is an old inquisitor of the church who mixed with the Dark Order." Another guard walked in, pulling the first guard away. "He is a nasty disease who spits in your mouth if you get too close. God knows what kind of sickness is he carrying on him?" The guard sounded disgusted.

Dark Order.

Aston grabbed his head. There was something about this word which triggered something in his mind and when he tried to recall it, he got an intense headache. A headache that he didn't invite, and then he forgot everything.

An unconscious man couldn't recall anything, right?

CHAPTER 6: THE PLOT

Aston dragged his feet behind the two guards that led him toward the execution ground, his worn boots scraping against the cobblestones. The sun had set down, leaving a dim moon hanging in the air like a tarnished silver coin, and they were going through the long-winded alleys where no one stayed. The occasional rat scurried away at their approach, disappearing into the shadows between abandoned market stalls.

Did it even matter? He was getting executed in a few minutes, or hours, and he didn't care about anything. For once he had a hope that he would be back next to his girlfriend in his apartment once the original prince's body hang to death. Maybe the hope helped him clear his mind.

Otherwise, it would be alarming to be this sharp and clear about one's thought on the day of execution.

Or was it mana, and the joy he had while playing with it in the last two days.

Two more steel plated hulks joined their entourage, their armor clanking with each step as they headed away from the normal route. Their footsteps echoed off the narrow walls, leaving no chance of escape for Aston. Not that he planned to do anything as he lacked the basic of energy, his limbs heavy as lead.

"Pick up the pace, prince," one of the guards growled, yanking roughly at the chains.

Aston stumbled forward, catching himself before he fell. "I'm moving as fast as I can," he muttered, earning himself a sharp jab in the ribs from another guard's gauntleted hand.

These fuck-faces. They didn't even give him a decent meal on the last day of his life.

"You might be a prince in the castle, but if we dump you in the Lanes of Lost City, no one will notice it," a guard whispered, his cold stinky breath brushing against Aston's neck. The stench of rotting meat and cheap ale made Aston's stomach turn. "We can just carry your head and tell the other prince that we executed you on the way."

He knew how these guards thought - petty men who lived a gutter-life and relished any scrap of power they could grasp. This one must be feeling particularly mighty while taking a prince under his shackles, savoring every moment of supposed dominance. But the original prince whose memories lived in Aston's mind was well versed in mind-games like these. Years of court intrigue and dealing with power-hungry nobles had taught him how to weather such provocations with dignity. That hard-earned wisdom helped Aston resist the urge to fight back against these peasants, knowing it would only give them the satisfaction they craved.

And he won't fucking let them have any satisfaction when he was about to die.

Aston flinched. Not at the cold voice of the guard, but someone was approaching them from a distance, and the guards hadn't noticed it yet. The mana flow of the surrounding was disturbed. Aston could see it clearly, but the guards couldn't. They wouldn't as they lacked the mana portals which Aston had five of them.

Despite not forming a spell circle, they had their usage, and Aston could harness some mana from the surrounding, allowing him heightened senses, and energy replenishment. It wasn't evident inside the prison as the walls were carved with anti-magic runes, but outside he could feel the power radiating through his mana portals into his body. The familiar tingle of energy coursed through his veins, making his fingertips buzz with renewed strength.

However, he also knew this was useless because he didn't know how to channel this power through his fingers. As per the original prince's memories mana portal allowed one to channel the energy, but a mana circle was something that turned the mana into a spell or usable entity. Without a mana circle on his body, he couldn't do anything.

A body flew from the space on the left and hurled into the stone wall next to him. The stone wall crumbled, and a man in his forties with a burned beard lay over it, his gut split open, exposing a palm-sized spell circle.

The circle shone with mana flow - blue and purple which amused Aston. The spell circle looked quite simple in his eyes, like the carving on the wooden furniture.

Another man flew from the left and surprisingly, it was Sir Rodric, his right hand glowing like a volcano in the shadows of the night.

"Prince, we meet again." Sir Rodric landed next to him, his right arm still radiating heat that Aston could feel against his skin. Wisps of smoke curled from Sir Rodric's fingers, carrying the acrid scent of burned flesh. "I never thought the frantic of Dark Order would come to save you, or kill you. Or was it your plan from the start? A final burst before dying?" he asked menacingly, taking a step closer, his boots crunching on the scattered debris.

Aston ignored Sir Rodric's towering presence, his eyes still on the corpse of the man lying on the ground. It looked interesting. And the more interesting thing was the old woman hiding in the shadows. Sir Rodric had come prepared. Even if Aston had the power to escape from four guards, he would have never escaped two magicians.

"Answer the Sir." A guard poked Aston with his metal rod.

Aston almost snapped back at the guard, but when he saw the way Sir Rodric looked at him, too eager for his defiance, he calmed down. The old knight's dark brown eyes gleamed with anticipation, his fingers twitching. Then he noticed someone in the shadows, ready to strike at any moment - another figure lurking just beyond the torchlight's reach.

There were more things at stake here, and if he played it carefully he might have a chance to survive through this. His mind raced through possibilities, weighing each potential response against what he knew of the bald warrior's temperament and the unseen threats surrounding him.

Everything hung in his reaction. One wrong word, one misplaced gesture, and he knew the metal rods wouldn't be the worst of his problems.

CHAPTER 7: THE POWER OF SPELL CIRCLE

The eerie silence and the dim lights from the torches made the shadows dance in the streets of the Lost City. The ancient stone walls seemed to breathe with each flicker of flame, creating phantoms that twisted and writhed in the darkness.

Aston licked his dry, cracked lips, pondering on the words, his mind racing with thoughts. Sweat trickled down his neck despite the cool night air. He had to play this carefully to get a chance of survival, knowing that one wrong word could seal his fate. Somehow, he had to get to the execution grounds without getting killed. If only he could meet his father, the king, he might have a glimmer of hope.

"Sir Rodric, is this how your guards behave with a prince?" Aston replied, forcing a rage through his eyes that he didn't entirely feel. His voice carried the practiced authority of royal breeding. "Although I'm getting executed, I'm still a prince, and you shouldn't let a mere guard poke a prince. How are you going to answer my father about this?" He watched the muscular knight's dark brown eyes for any reaction, studying the way his long beard twitched. If only he kept his demeanor, Sir Rodric wouldn't play underhanded tricks and kill him right away. The weight of the moment pressed down on him like a physical force.

Sir Rodric chuckled. his beard swaying in the evening winds. "A prince on death bed is nothing but a trash for a guard. A treacherous prince who joined criminals. Even if you had prepared an army to save you, it wouldn't have mattered. I knew about your plans since you asked to meet me through Gra'pa."

Sir Rodric continued. "There are ten magicians surrounding this area. Majesty has ordered us to get this done in darkness, so no one would know you ever lived." His dark brown eyes gleamed with a predatory satisfaction. "These Dark Order bastards will all die under my hands. Mark my word, prince, they will all die along with you."

Dark Order. The words triggered an avalanche of fragments in Aston's mind, like shards of a broken mirror slowly piecing themselves together. They belonged to the original prince, memories he hadn't accessed before. The taste of bitter tea during secret meetings, whispered conversations in candlelit rooms, the rustle of papers bearing plans to expose corrupt officials.

No - it was more than that. It was a bloody conspiracy against the king.

And there was more - a connection he hadn't seen before. The Dark Order wasn't just a reformative organization; it was a movement born from desperation. They sought to wrestle power from the current king, who ruled with the church's blessing and crushed opposition with military might. Their vision was radical: a government chosen by the common people, for the common people.

"You're awfully quiet, Prince," Sir Rodric said, flexing his still-glowing fingers. "Remembering old friends?"

The fragments kept coming, but they were jumbled, like a puzzle missing crucial pieces. The original prince's betrayal of his father, the secret meetings, the moment of discovery - all of it swirled in Aston's mind, but the complete picture remained frustratingly out of reach.

There was a lot to unpack here, and Aston's pulse quickened as he assessed just how deep in trouble he was. The original prince had methodically dug his own grave, and then died, yanking Aston from Earth straight into this political inferno he never asked to be part of. Each revelation felt like another weight pressing down on his shoulders, threatening to crush him beneath its burden.

Something about Sir Rodric's casual demeanor felt wrong. A prickle of unease ran down Aston's spine, making the hair on the back of his neck stand on end. The ambush felt too...convenient. The way Rodric spoke, the almost eager glint in his dark brown eyes as he mentioned the Dark Order, the satisfied way he stroked his long beard... A chilling realization began to dawn, spreading like ice through Aston's veins. Had he been played from the start? Was *this* why Rodric had agreed to meet? To draw them out? He was bait, dangled expertly by a master manipulator with over a century of experience in such games.

He could clearly see Sir Rodric's plan now, the pieces falling into place with devastating clarity. The reason the Sir Rodric agreed to meet him must have been to draw out the Dark Order people supporting the original prince, but Aston hadn't been aware of this connection at the time. So, nothing happened then. The Dark Order people must have become desperate to either save Aston or kill him, so they sent a few helpers who walked straight into Sir Rodric's carefully laid trap. Now one lay dead before him, a stark reminder of the deadly stakes in this game of power and deception.

Sir Rodric was playing all along and he had no plans to trade anything with him.

In fact, the king might be behind all of this. There was no way the king would have pardoned him. Not even in the wildest dream.

Damn it all! His fingers curled into fists. Why did that entitled fool had to push things this far and create such a mess?

"Prince," Sir Rodric's deep voice rumbled through the chamber, his beard quivering with barely contained anger, "you went against the majesty and there is no pardon from it. I don't know why you thought you could strike a deal with me, but no way I would ever support the Dark Order." His weathered hand rested on the pommel of his sword, a silent threat.

Or was it more of a performance for the woman standing in the dark? Aston could guess who she was from the original prince's memories.

However, there were more important things at play here.

Aston's attention was drawn to the spell circle as it dissipated into wisps of blue light, watching intently as the mana drained from the dead man's cooling body. The intricate lines carved into the mana portal grew fainter with each passing moment. The realization hit him like a physical blow - the reason he couldn't create a spell circle wasn't lack of knowledge, but lack of foundation. He had no platform to carve the circle on. A literal platform. But that didn't mean he had no way of carving a spell circle.

This changed everything. A plan began forming in his mind, dangerous but possible.

"Sir Rodric, you are wrong in one thing," Aston said as he squatted down next to the remains of the Dark Order magician, his fingers dancing in the shadows, collecting the mana threads from the air.

Sir Rodric's dark eyes narrowed, his century-old face creasing with suspicion. "What might that be, prince?"

Aston pulled the mana threads inside his right palm, moving them toward the mana portal. Each thread acted like a needle and he began carving the same circle he had seen on the corpse's mana portal. He had played with this before, and if he could pull it out, then he might be saved from this predicament.

"What are you doing, prince? Pacifying your dead friend."

Aston chuckled without wavering his attention from his own mana portal.

With practiced concentration, he began recreating the spell circle he'd witnessed inside the dead man's body, carefully etching it into his palm where his first mana portal resided. The mana threads danced and twisted around the portal, forming intricate wave patterns that threatened to dissolve like smoke in the wind. Sweat beaded on his forehead as he fought to complete the circle before it could fade. Just as the last line connected, a powerful surge of mana erupted from his mana portal, manifesting as a crystalline shield of swirling water that encompassed his body.

"Magic, that's magic." Sir Rodric stepped back.

Aston smiled, but he could feel the tiredness seeping into his bones. The process only took a few seconds, but he felt like he had worked in the desert for days without any water.

"You learned the magic. That's impossible. That's a heretic method." Sir Rodric muttered, his weathered face pale with disbelief. Orange flames danced between his fingers, casting flickering shadows across his ancient features. "No one can learn a spell circle that quickly. You have done something heretic."

"It's not important, Sir Rodric," Aston said, keeping his voice steady despite his racing heart. "The important thing is that I'm a magician now. Right, Bishop Aganstha?" he asked, staring into the darkness where the old woman stood.

"You used a cheating method. You are not a magician." Sir Rodric complained.

Aston could feel his frustration because this would change everything. It would open up a chance for him to survive. Magicians were treated differently from the commoners, and even the king couldn't execute them easily.

"Bishop, you are there, witnessing me." He coughed. "Anyone who can cast a spell in front of the Bishop is given entry into the Society of Magicians," Aston said in a firm voice, recalling all the details behind the working of the church. Original prince was a fool to go against the king and church, but he was a very studious person, and he had learned all the things about the church and the workings of the Society of Magicians.

That's how he planned the coup, the resurgence, with the help of the Dark Order.

"I never thought a prince with five mana portals would be a dud." Bishop Aganstha walked out of the shadows, her silver hair gleaming like polished steel. "It's sufficient for your entry, but that doesn't warrant you a pleading. Your crime will still give you a death penalty." She arched her brows.

Aston chuckled. "What if I expose the whereabouts of the Dark Order to my father in return for pardon?" He released his tenuous hold on the spell circle, and the water shield dissolved into a fine mist that dampened the surrounding air.

"You will do that?" Bishop arched her brows, a faint smile hanging on her face.

Aston nodded. "You can pardon me when you wind up everyone from their order." Bishop will accept his suggestion because it will allow her to gain a footing in the church's higher order.

"Indeed, it's sufficient," she said, her smile creating a web of wrinkles across her face. She clasped her hands before her ceremonial robes. "And with your promise, I'm sure the king will give you pardon, Prince Aston."

Aston released a heavy sigh that seemed to carry the weight of two souls - one mourning the betrayal of the original prince's cherished values, the other embracing the promise of a new life. His fingers traced the lingering warmth of the spell circle on his palm.

Was it worth betraying the original prince's values? The question echoed in his mind like a distant bell, and only time could provide the answer he sought.

CHAPTER 8: MESSAGE FROM THE CAPITAL

E^{lara} Elara Thistlewood slapped the book on the table, sending a cloud of dust flying around the office. It had been only a day since the servant hadn't come, and could already draw a picture with her fingers.

Getting up, she moved close to the window, watching the sunlight streaming through the gap in the wooden doors. Tiny particles of the dust danced like tiny stars in the streams of sunlight.

Pinching the nose between her fingers, she stopped the sneeze. She would hate dirtying her pristine green dress today, its embroidered hem still crisp from morning pressing. However, she had to get rid of the dust as well. The overwhelming dust had muted her smelling senses, and she wanted to smell fresh lavender and chamomile she had brought from her estate this morning. The flowers sat in a crystal vase, their beauty wasted in this grimy environment.

"Gosta, what happened to Maria? Why isn't she here already?" she asked and the guard standing outside the door rushed in, his broken sword dangling over his waist, the metal making a distinctive clinking sound against his belt buckle. "And why isn't your sword fixed yet? How would it look when the mayor's guard has a broken sword?"

Gosta shifted uncomfortably, his weathered face showing signs of exhaustion. Gosta was a grizzled old man, well into his two-hundreds, his nose flattened not by age, as he claimed, but by fights from his youth. A subtle twitch in his left eye betrayed years of service, while deep creases framed his mouth. The scars crisscrossing his knuckles spoke more truth of his rough past than he ever did.

"Forgive me, Lord Mayor. But Maria is sick and can't move. The magical insects are rampaging in the town and common people can't do anything about them." Gosta brushed his fingers over the hilt of the broken sword, the leather wrapping worn thin from years of use. "Lord Mayor, if you can ask for a healer from the Lord Governor, we might survive this summer, else we might lose it."

"And how many more have fallen ill?" Elara demanded, her voice sharp with concern.

"Three more since yesterday, my lady. The baker's youngest and two field workers."

Elara slammed her palm on the table, sending the remaining dust flying away. She didn't care about her dress anymore. The table looked cleaner but some maps of dust lines remained behind, like ghostly trails of her frustration.

"Gosta, if I could fix everything then I would have already done that." Elara replied calmly, but inside her heart a fury of pain surged through, smashing her emotions around. She stood and walked to the window, watching the townspeople hurry about their business below, each one a responsibility weighing on her conscience. She had tried to plead her case to Lord Governor hundred times, but since she failed to provide the required mine output Lord Governor had turned away from the town of Valtoria, and she had no solution for this. Her fingers traced the cool glass of the window as she fought back tears of frustration.

"Perhaps," she whispered, more to herself than to Gosta, "it's time we looked for help elsewhere."

"Lord Mayor, there is message arrived from the capital." Nadia, the second guard, stepped through. She looked much more presentable than Gosta clad in metal armor, her confident smile reflecting on her newest spell circle, but she lacked the maturity of Gosta who served her for last ten years, and before that her father, the previous Lord Mayor.

"Nadia, you have to ask for permission before walking in." Gosta muttered under his breath, shifting his weight with a creak of weathered leather.

"It's fine, for now," Elara said, reaching with her hand. A message from the capital - it sounded important. Much higher than her paygrade. This was the first time she would be handling something from the capital itself.

"Yes, Lord Mayor. There is a message from the capital." Nadia blinked, her brown eyes twinkling under the dim light coming from the window. She had a muscular frame, and taller than Gosta, but she hunched when she walked and looked smaller than she was. The polished buckles of her armor caught the morning light, a stark contrast to her uncertain demeanor.

"And where is that message?" Elara frowned, feeling impatient. Another delay was the last thing she needed today.

"I forgot it in the message room." Nadia looked down, pushing the loose strands of her hair behind her ear. A faint blush crept across her cheeks as she shifted uncomfortably in her pristine armor.

"Then go and bring it here. Now." Elara shouted, her voice echoing off the stone walls. She pinched the bridge of her nose, instantly regretting her burst of anger. Too many things were going wrong since the morning. In fact, too many things were going wrong with the town, and she was failing to maintain her father's legacy.

Nadia's boots clattered against the floorboards as she dashed out. The sound of her hurried footsteps faded down the corridor. She came back in a mere minute, slightly out of breath, her armor clanking with each movement. The message room was nothing but a common room the guards used to keep their books, and eat their food.

In a small town, mayor's house was merely a two story building with creaking stairs and weathered walls, and she couldn't designate too many rooms for the functions the office barely served. Messaging was one of them.

Nadia handed her a brown parchment, the thick paper rough against Elara's fingers. It had the seal of the capital, a black dragon with intricate scales that seemed to catch the light.

With trembling fingers, she broke the seal, the wax crumbling slightly. As she read through it, the muscles in her jaw tightened, her frown deepening with each line.

"What the hell are they trying to do?" she glanced up at Gosta, the paper crinkling in her tightening grip.

"Nadia, please wait outside." Gosta's voice was gentle but firm as he signaled the young woman. She stepped out with a low nod, closing the door quietly behind her. "Lord Mayor, what happened?"

Elara scanned the old man who looked so much like her father in this moment - the same concerned furrow between his brows, the same steady presence. Gosta was the longest living elder of the town, and if she could trust anyone then it would be Gosta.

"Gosta, they are sending a prince to serve this town for a few years." She began pacing, her boots making soft thuds against the floor. "But why? It doesn't make sense."

"Is that Prince Aston, Lord Mayor?" Gosta's hand rested on the pommel of his sword, a habit he'd developed over decades of service.

Elara stopped pacing and arched her brows. "How do you know?"

"I heard about him." Gosta tapped on the sword's hilt, the metal making a soft ping. "He is trouble as per the rumors say. He has no Spell Circles, and I heard other princes were trying to get rid of him."

"But why send him here?" Elara slumped into her chair, the wood groaning under her weight. "Wouldn't he be better inside the king's palace? I bet the king can feed a useless prince."

"Something must have happened, and I don't think it's for anything good." Gosta sighed - a sigh heavy with worry that seemed to age him further. He moved to the window, looking out at the town below.

Elara's heart felt dampened. There was trouble every-where, and she could see no ray of hope for this town. The summer's approach loomed like a dark cloud, bringing with it the promise of destruction. She traced the edge of the parchment, lost in thought.

At least the exiled prince wasn't an option. Was there any option that would save this town and not make her destroy her father's legacy with her own hands?

CHAPTER 9: A NEW BEGINNING

The barren land stretched endlessly like a giant snake's tail under a harsh sun. Aston squinted through the carriage's sole window at the monotonous dirt road. He'd learned his lesson about riding up front with Fragriver - his ass still remembered those painful hours bouncing on the hard wooden seat.

Inside the coach, he traced his fingers through the air, following the invisible mana threads that danced like gossamer in the sunlight. They twisted and turned, forming patterns that changed with each passing moment. Some threads glowed faintly blue, others shimmered with a purply hue. Twenty-three days of study, and still they surprised him with new configurations.

"Fascinating," he muttered, weaving his fingers through a particularly complex knot of mana. The thread pulsed, then split into three distinct strands.

Another dust devil whirled across the road, and Aston quickly retreated from the window. The carriage's musty interior - all leather and old wood - wrapped around him like a familiar blanket. He wrinkled his nose at the stack of dry rations in the corner, their wrappings already showing signs of wear. Fragriver's mistake in packing had left them with food well past its prime.

He bet if not for the salt he had applied on the skin, the meat would have tasted like rotten shit already.

"Prince," Fragriver's voice rasped from above, each word seeming to scrape against his throat. "We will need three more days to reach the town of Valtoria."

Aston looked up at the ceiling, picturing the skeletal old man perched on his seat. The driver's wheezing had gotten worse over the past week, and his coughing fit more frequently.

Aston rubbed his palm over the twenty days' old beard and wondered if he would get this cleaned in the town he was exiled to.

"Thank you, Fragriver," he called back, trying to keep the concern from his voice. "Let's make camp by the river tonight. You need proper rest." He glanced at the horses' shadows stretching alongside the carriage. "We've pushed hard enough today."

A wet, hacking cough was his only response, making Aston's stomach churn. He had never learned to handle horses, let alone guide them through this desolate landscape. The thought of reaching Valtoria alone seemed scary all of a sudden.

Yes, he was exiled by his father to manage the town of Valtoria - a backwater town in the kingdom of Drakonia which neighbored an ancient mountain that no one had conquered yet. But he had half expected this after giving out the little information he had on the Dark Order. His new identity as a magician and a traitor son had only gained him an exile in the remote town, and he was fine as long as he didn't get killed. He wasn't the real prince to have any familiar ties with the king, or other prince and princesses.

They could all burn in hell or die from eating shit and he wouldn't care.

The only issue was the tracking device planted around his ankle. It was a magician thing, and if he didn't know he was in a medieval world, he would have thought they bought it from the modern earth's prison. The metal band chafed against his skin, a constant reminder of his father's distrust.

"Fuck, they could have just asked me to go to another kingdom, and I'd have obliged."

Suddenly, he glanced at the dance of mana threads. The knot he was trying to fix had undone itself, the silvery strands twisting and writhing like serpents in the afternoon light. They kept forming and loosening up on themselves like a mystery, and he loved watching it when it happened. A couple of times he even thought he saw a magic circle forming naturally, but before it could form, the mana threads moved on their own, dissipating the magic pressure forming in the air with a soft hiss.

This time as well a circle had formed. A circle in the outer sense, but he could see the mana threads tying around each other, forming a pattern, unique and beautiful. The threads glowed with an inner light, pulsing like a heartbeat against the darkened inside of the coach.

Could he use it to form a spell circle on his second mana portal?

"Nothing ventured..." he whispered, his breath creating small puffs in the cooling air. He hadn't tried it, but what would happen if he failed? Nothing. The last spell circle, Water Shield, had faded away after he let go, and he could form it again later on the same mana portal.

It was worth a try. Even Picasso needed a thousand tries before inventing the light bulb.

Wait, was it Galileo?

Whatever.

Squinting, Aston began carving the same mana circle he was seeing in nature on his second mana portal under the left palm. The mana threads danced across the semi-wax like mana portal, leaving traces of warmth against his skin, and he soon managed to form half of the circle. Sweat beads fell down his forehead as he focused everything on this task. This mana portal seemed more difficult than the first one, but he didn't give up and continued carving the spell circle.

Then the circle in the air dissipated, the mana threads going their own ways. Aston paused before continuing carving the spell circle. He remembered the generic formation and he carved it - one thread at a time.

"Just a little more," he urged himself, feeling the familiar tingle of a magic building beneath his palm.

Before he carved the last line, he took a deep breath. Sweat trickled down his temple as his fingers trembled slightly. This was still uncharted territory, and the magical energy pulsing around him felt different - wilder, more unpredictable.

Fuck it!

Aston carved the final line on the second mana portal with a swift, decisive motion. Immediately, a surge of power coursed through his body like liquid fire. He felt an illusion enveloping him, his vision blurring at the edges, before he violently coughed up a mouthful of metallic-tasting blood and pitched forward into darkness.

The next time he opened his eyes, he found himself lying on a comfortable bed, the mattress soft beneath his aching body. Four dimly lit walls surrounded him, their wooden panels gleaming softly in the low light. A faint scent of jasmine wafted through the air, mingling with the sharp tang of medicinal herbs.

What the fuck happened? He rubbed his face, wincing as every movement of his arm sent waves of piercing pain through his muscles, like thousands of needles pricking his skin.

"Anyone... around?" he tried to shout, but the words emerged as a raspy whisper from his parched throat.

Fragriver - the old bony coach driver - rushed through the door - surprisingly agile for his age and form. His weathered face breaking into a relieved smile, worry lines still creasing his forehead. "Prince, you are finally awake!" He hurried to Aston's bedside, wringing his gnarled hands. "I would have killed myself if you hadn't woken up soon. We've been beside ourselves with worry."

"What happened?" Aston asked, his tongue feeling like sandpaper.

Fragriver poured a glass of water from a nearby pitcher, his hands shaking slightly. "You fell in the coach when we were three days away. When I looked inside..." He paused, swallowing hard. "There was blood everywhere, my Prince. You looked like you had spilled every single drop from inside you. What happened? Did someone attack you? But I didn't see no one, not a soul on the road."

Aston accepted the water gratefully, rubbing his forehead as he recalled what really happened. The spell circle, the surge of power, then nothing but darkness. He frowned, glancing inwardly to examine his energy network. A fading spell circle glowed dimly on his left palm mana portal. It could be activated once more, but would it exact the same bloody toll?

Somehow, deep in his gut, he felt it wouldn't. Taking a deep breath, he activated it. An illusion materialized before him: a woman, strikingly beautiful in her twenties, walked through the door. In the vision, she welcomed him, introducing herself as Elara Thistlewood, mayor of Valtoria.

The illusion dissipated like morning mist, and moments later, the same beautiful woman from his vision strode into the room. Her presence commanded attention, her emerald dress rustling softly as she moved.

And her eyes - they were breathtaking.

"Prince, you are finally awake." Her smile was radiant but measured, professional.

"And you are?" Aston asked, though he already knew the answer.

"I'm Elara Thistlewood," she said, her lips curling in a smile.

"Elara..." Aston scanned her.

"Mayor Elara, prince."

She executed a perfect bow, showing proper respect. However, there was an unmistakable hint of dissatisfaction in her tone that pricked at his pride like a needle.

Yet Aston barely registered her subtle emotions, his mind reeling from the implications of what his spell circle had accomplished. It had shown him a minute into the future with perfect clarity. Time magic - actual time magic.

Fucking time magic.

Was it even possible?

This changed everything. Everything.

Excitedly, Aston pushed his mana into the second spell circle and the images changed, someone was coming, shouting for help.

Trouble was coming.

CHAPTER 10: EPILOGUE

"You saw what?" An ethereal figure in the prison ceiling floated in and out, its translucent form rippling like smoke against the damp stone. Moonlight filtered through its essence, casting strange patterns on the moldy floor.

"A Mana Traveler. He can control mana threads in the air. I saw him weaving them like silver spiderwebs," the old man's eyes glazed over with the memory, his gnarled fingers tracing invisible patterns in the air.

"You are an old fool. Those kinds are banished from the land." The ethereal figure whispered, its voice like wind through dead leaves. It drifted closer, its form condensing briefly before dispersing again. "The purge made sure of that."

"I don't know. I might have seen some illusions." The old man scratched his matted beard, doubt creeping into his voice. "The prison walls play tricks sometimes."

"Isn't it time for you to get out of this place and work to raise your clan?" the ethereal figure asked, circling around the old man's hunched form. "Your people need you more than these cold stones do."

"Not yet. I've to wait for him to appear. The fate tells about this node in the land. He will come here. One day or another." The old man said before diving into the scraps of bones he loved to munch on. The sound of his teeth grinding against the calcified remains echoed through the cell, making the ethereal figure recoil in disgust.

"Your obsession will be the death of you," the figure muttered, beginning to fade into nothingness. "Just like it was for so many others."

The old man didn't respond, too busy sorting through his precious bone collection, his eyes gleaming with an unsettling intensity in the darkness.

Aston's story will continue in the next book and he will come soon. You can sign up to my email list to receive a free short story and hear about the release before anyone else.

Get the Free Story: Dream Realm.

Milton Keynes UK
Ingram Content Group UK Ltd.
UKHW030900151124
451262UK00001B/21